Written by M...
Designed b...
Cover and package de...

Copyright © 2015, 2018 by Scholastic In...
in 2015 by Tangerine Press. All rights reserved. P... ...c., *Publishers since 1920.*
SCHOLASTIC and associated logos are trademarks and/or registered trademarks of Scholastic Inc.

The publisher does not have any control over and does not assume any responsibility for author or third-party websites or their content.

No part of this publication may be reproduced, stored in a retrieval system, or transmitted in any form or by any means, electronic, mechanical, photocopying, recording, or otherwise, without written permission of the publisher. For information regarding permission, write to Scholastic Inc., Attention: Permissions Department, 557 Broadway, New York, NY 10012.

This book is a work of fiction. Names, characters, places, and incidents are either the product of the author's imagination or are used fictitiously, and any resemblance to actual persons, living or dead, business establishments, events, or locales is entirely coincidental.

10 9 8 7 6 5 4 3 2 1   18 19 20 21 22

ISBN 978-1-338-32301-6

Printed and bound in Jiaxing, China   68

SCHOLASTIC
scholastic.com

Photos ©: box paper scrap: t_kimura/iStockphoto; box water: ddbell/iStockphoto; box shark fins: SSSCCC/iStockphoto; box sharks: ap-images/iStockphoto; cover main: Mike Parry/Getty Images; back cover water: Maks Narodenko/Shutterstock, Inc.; 1 background: Andrey_Kuzmin/Shutterstock, Inc.; 2 main: Jim Abernethy/Getty Images; 3 top: www.Narchuk.com/Getty Images; 3 top paper: SCOTTCHAN/Shutterstock, Inc.; 3 center top: Creation/Shutterstock, Inc.; 3 center bottom: Jim Abernethy/Getty Images; 3 bottom: Chris Ross/Getty Images; 3 background: Jim Abernethy/Getty Images; 4 background: CoreyFord/iStockphoto; 4 bottom left: STILLFX/Shutterstock, Inc.; 4 bottom right: STILLFX/iStockphoto; 5 center: Catmando/Shutterstock, Inc.; 5 bottom teeth: Masterfile; 5 bottom left: donatas1205/Shutterstock, Inc.; 5 background: CoreyFord/iStockphoto; 6 background: Chris Ross/Getty Images; 6 bottom: moyogo/Wikimedia; 6 center left: Josh Humbert/Getty Images; 7 top: etraveler/iStockphoto; 7 bottom: bonishphotography/iStockphoto; 7 paper scrap: xpixel/Shutterstock, Inc.; 7 background: Chris Ross/Getty Images; 7 center: Hilton Mantooth; 8 main: Ruth Petzold/Getty Images; 9 top: David Jenkins/Robert Harding World Imagery/Corbis Images; 9 background: Ruth Petzold/Getty Images; 10 main: Education Images/UIG; 11 bottom right: STILLFX/Shutterstock, Inc.; 11 bottom left: NaluPhoto/iStockphoto; 11 background: Education Images/UIG; 12 main: Education Images/UIG/Getty Images; 13 center left: Greg Amptman/Shutterstock, Inc.; 13 center left photo frames: rangizzz/Shutterstock, Inc.; 13 center right: STILLFX/Shutterstock, Inc.; 13 bottom left: Matt9122/Shutterstock, Inc.; 13 bottom right: Devonyu/iStockphoto; 13 background: Education Images/UIG/Getty Images; 14 main: Karen Doody/Stocktrek Images/Getty Images; 15 center: MP cz/Shutterstock, Inc.; 15 bottom: ZWEID/iStockphoto; 15 main: Karen Doody/Stocktrek Images/Getty Images; 15 bottom photo frame: SCOTTCHAN/Shutterstock, Inc.; 16 main: stephaniki2/iStockphoto; 17 top: qldian/iStockphoto; 17 center: qldian/iStockphoto; 17 bottom: CAlleaume/iStockphoto; 17 background: stephaniki2/iStockphoto; 17 photo frames: SCOTTCHAN/Shutterstock, Inc.; 18 main: Matt9122/Shutterstock, Inc.; 19 center left: Shane Gross/Shutterstock, Inc.; 19 bottom left: ilbusca/iStockphoto; 19 bottom right: Matt9122/Shutterstock, Inc.; 19 background: Matt9122/Shutterstock, Inc.; 19 photo frame: SCOTTCHAN/Shutterstock, Inc.; 19 paper scrap: xpixel/Shutterstock, Inc.; 20 main: stephaniki2/iStockphoto; 21 top: UWphotographer/iStockphoto; 21 bottom right: JudiLen/iStockphoto; 21 bottom left: ShaneGross/iStockphoto; 21 background: stephaniki2/iStockphoto; 21 photo frames: SCOTTCHAN/Shutterstock, Inc.; 22 main: Alexander Sofonov/Barcroft Media/Getty Images; 23 center: Tui De Roy/Getty Images; 23 bottom: kamonchanok5211224102/iStockphoto; 23 background: Alexander Sofonov/Barcroft Media/Getty Images; 23 photo frame: SCOTTCHAN/Shutterstock, Inc.; 24 background: BryanToro/iStockphoto; 24 bottom: bonishphotography/iStockphoto; 24 photo frame: SCOTTCHAN/Shutterstock, Inc.; 25 center: Brian J. Skerry/Getty Images; 25 bottom: Mark Conlin/Getty Images; 25 background: BryanToro/iStockphoto; 25 photo frame: SCOTTCHAN/Shutterstock, Inc.; 26 main: Jim Abernethy/Getty Images; 27 bottom: NaluPhoto/iStockphoto; 27 background: Jim Abernethy/Getty Images; 27 photo frame: SCOTTCHAN/Shutterstock, Inc.; 28 background: dioch/Shutterstock, Inc.; 28 top: Entienou/iStockphoto; 28 center left: Stephen Frink/Getty Images; 28 center right: Steven Trainoff Ph.D./Getty Images; 29 top: atese/iStockphoto; 29 bottom: BlueRingMedia/Shutterstock, Inc.; 29 background: dioch/Shutterstock, Inc.; 30 background: Willyam Bradbery/Shutterstock, Inc.; 31 top: david olah/iStockphoto; 31 center top: bgton/iStockphoto; 31 center bottom: Fox Photos/Getty Images; 31 bottom left: Raphael Christinat/Shutterstock, Inc.; 31 bottom right: Anastasios71/Shutterstock, Inc.; 31 background: Willyam Bradbery/Shutterstock, Inc.; 31 photo frame: SCOTTCHAN/Shutterstock, Inc.; 32 background: Swimwitdafishes/iStockphoto; 32 paper scrap: xpixel/Shutterstock, Inc.

Attack and fatality statistics are from the International Shark Attack File (ISAF), Florida Museum of Natural History, University of Florida. All statistics are for unprovoked attacks.

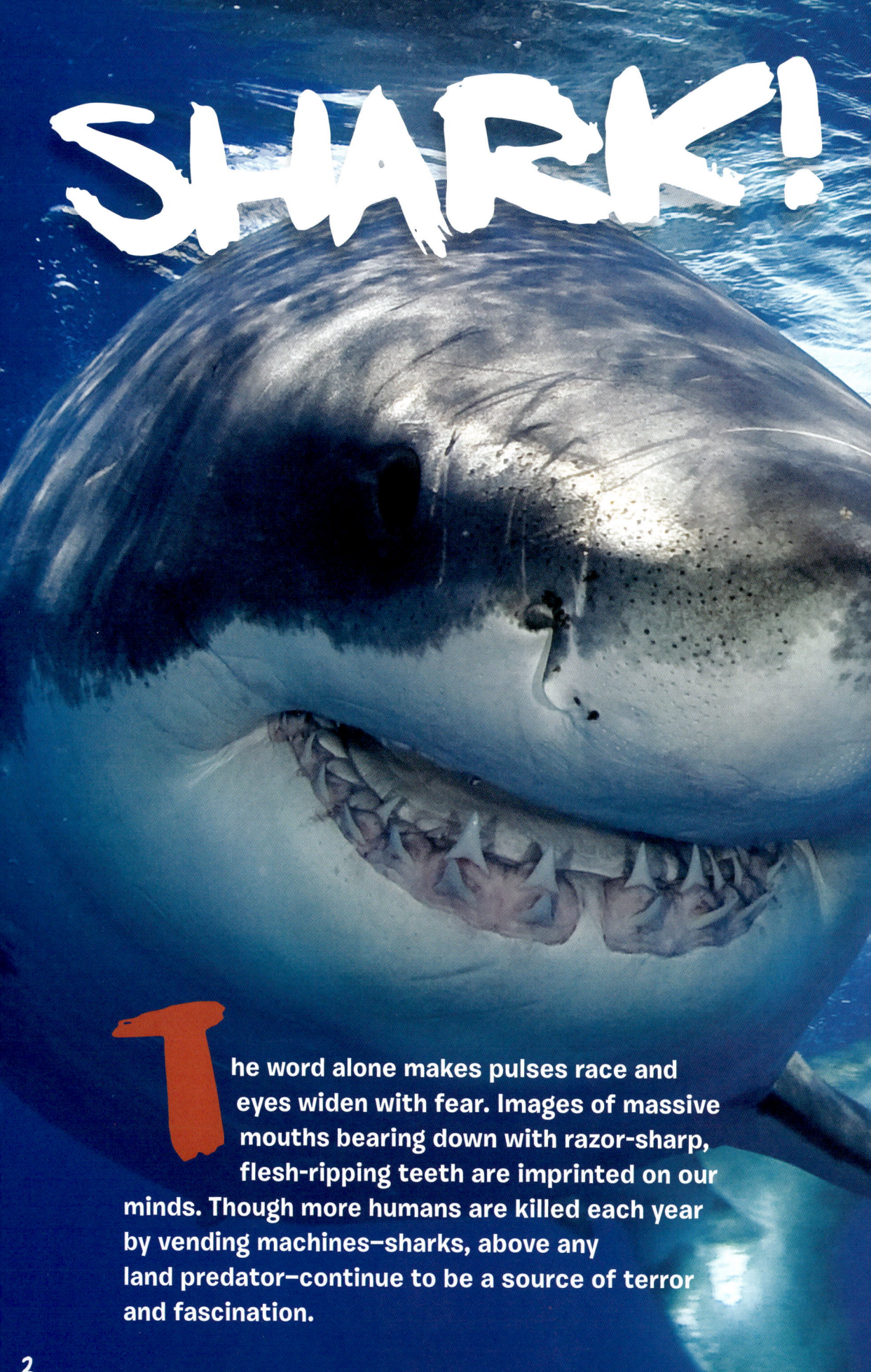

SHARK!

The word alone makes pulses race and eyes widen with fear. Images of massive mouths bearing down with razor-sharp, flesh-ripping teeth are imprinted on our minds. Though more humans are killed each year by vending machines—sharks, above any land predator—continue to be a source of terror and fascination.

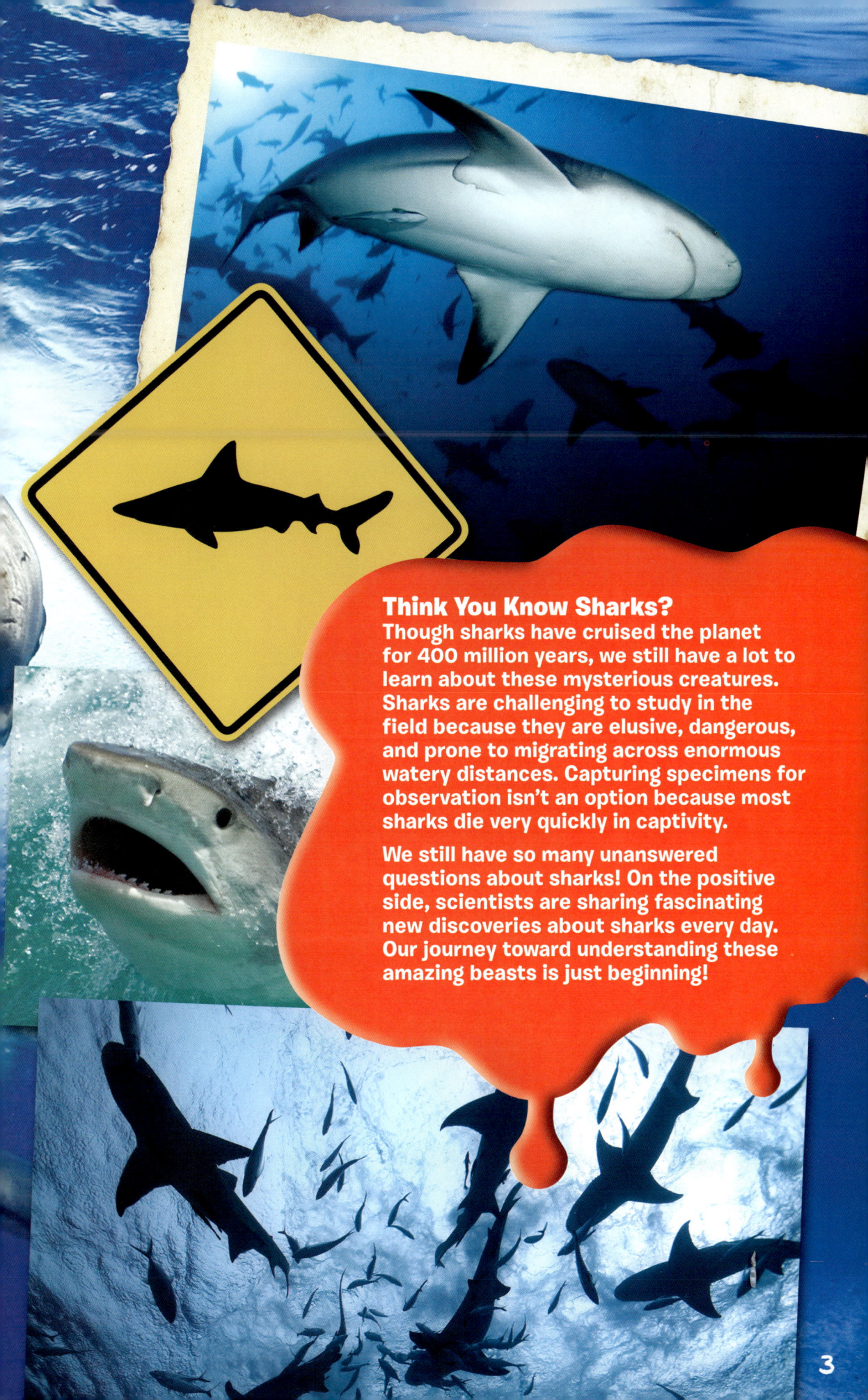

Think You Know Sharks?
Though sharks have cruised the planet for 400 million years, we still have a lot to learn about these mysterious creatures. Sharks are challenging to study in the field because they are elusive, dangerous, and prone to migrating across enormous watery distances. Capturing specimens for observation isn't an option because most sharks die very quickly in captivity.

We still have so many unanswered questions about sharks! On the positive side, scientists are sharing fascinating new discoveries about sharks every day. Our journey toward understanding these amazing beasts is just beginning!

MEGAL

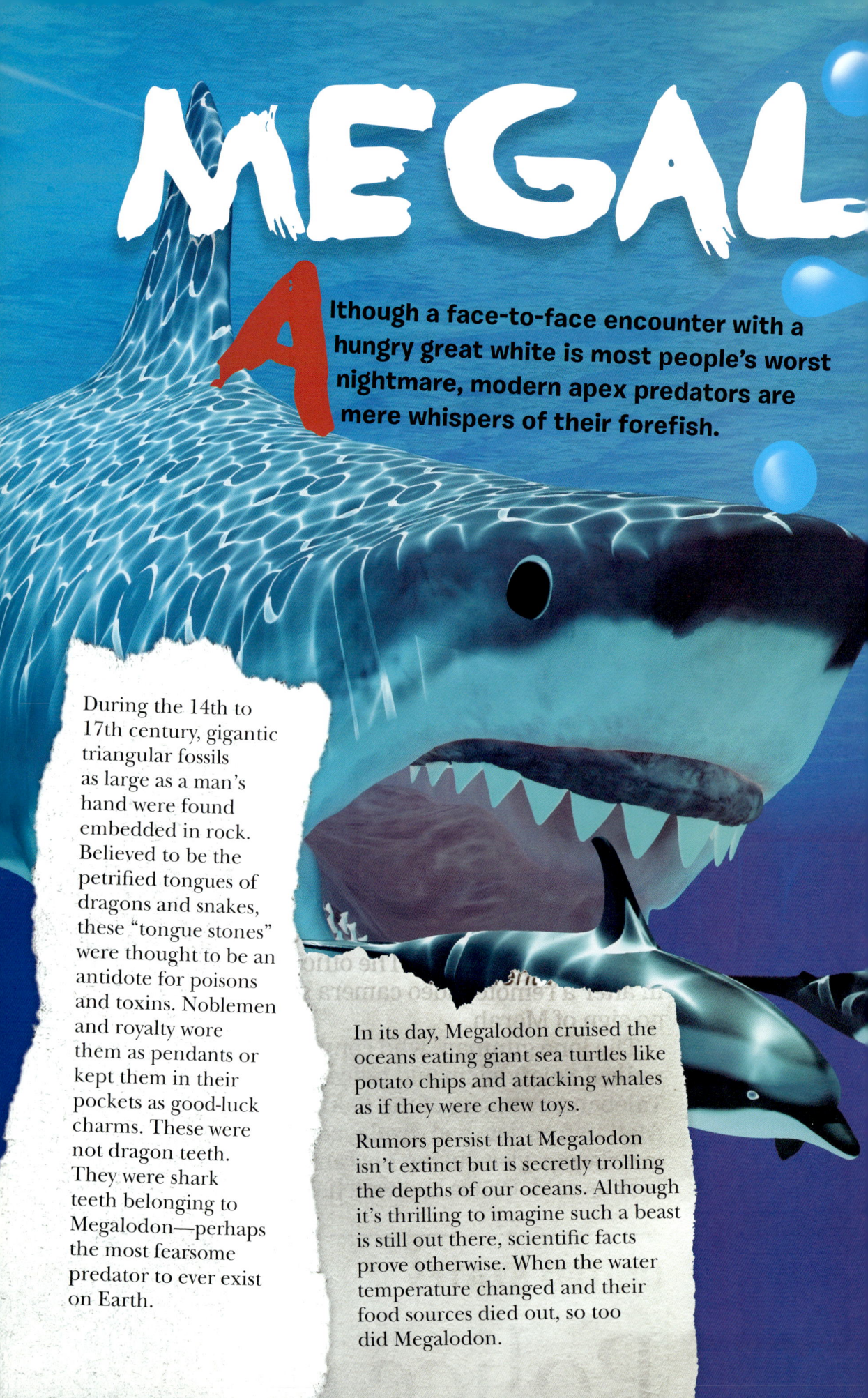

Although a face-to-face encounter with a hungry great white is most people's worst nightmare, modern apex predators are mere whispers of their forefish.

During the 14th to 17th century, gigantic triangular fossils as large as a man's hand were found embedded in rock. Believed to be the petrified tongues of dragons and snakes, these "tongue stones" were thought to be an antidote for poisons and toxins. Noblemen and royalty wore them as pendants or kept them in their pockets as good-luck charms. These were not dragon teeth. They were shark teeth belonging to Megalodon—perhaps the most fearsome predator to ever exist on Earth.

In its day, Megalodon cruised the oceans eating giant sea turtles like potato chips and attacking whales as if they were chew toys.

Rumors persist that Megalodon isn't extinct but is secretly trolling the depths of our oceans. Although it's thrilling to imagine such a beast is still out there, scientific facts prove otherwise. When the water temperature changed and their food sources died out, so too did Megalodon.

ODON *(Carcharodon megalodon)*

Lived:
15.9 million–2.6 million years ago during the Cenozoic Era (middle Miocene to end of Pliocene)

Claim to Fame:
Largest marine predator EVER

Size:
Length: Estimates range from 52–80 ft (16–24 m)
Weight: Estimates range from 53–114 tons (48–103 metric tons)

Distinguishing Characteristics:
A huge, stocky body with a giant mouth full of enormous teeth. Picture a mouth with fins.

Habitat:
Megalodon is believed to have hunted all the oceans in a wide range of marine environments—no region was spared its voracious appetite!

Diet:
Whales, dolphins, sea turtles, land creatures taking a dip

Hunting Style:
1. Open mouth
2. Swallow prey

Natural Predators: NONE

> A shark loses and replaces around 35,000 teeth over its lifespan.

Without a skeleton, scientists can only make educated guesses about Megalodon's size based on the similarity of the fossilized teeth to those of today's great white. Reaching lengths more than 7 in (17.78 cm), Megalodon teeth are the same shape and have the same serrated edges as the great white. Scientists have differing theories about Megalodon's size. At this point, we just don't know which one is correct.

Because shark skeletons are made of cartilage (the flexible connective tissue that makes your ears bendy), and cartilage breaks down over time, all that remains of prehistoric sharks are their teeth.

THE DANGER ZONE

Most unprovoked shark attacks happen off the Atlantic coast of Florida in the United States. Australia has the second highest number of attacks, followed by South Africa. These rankings are not concrete, however, because attacks in South Africa are not documented as they are elsewhere. Despite having the highest number of recorded attacks, only about 16 attacks occur per year in the United States, and one fatality every two years.

Map of World's Unprovoked Shark Attacks 1580–2014:

- 500 or more
- 200-499
- 40-199
- 1-39

Last updated Feb 20, 2014, International Shark Attack File, Florida Museum of Natural History, University of Florida

Though movies such as *Jaws* and shows from *Shark Week* make it look like sharks are hungry for human blood, the truth is we don't have the fat-to-bone ratio that a shark looks for in a tasty snack. Most shark attacks on humans are a case of mistaken identity. Unfortunately, such powerful jaws and sharp teeth mean a tiny taste test can result in fatal or disfiguring bites to a human body.

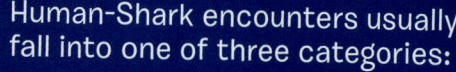

Human-Shark encounters usually fall into one of three categories:

The "Hit and Run" Attack: The most common type of encounter; the shark mistakes a human for prey and takes a bite, realizes its mistake, then releases and retreats. Often the victim does not even see the shark.

The "Bump and Bite" Attack: The shark circles the victim and gives it an exploratory bump, then moves in for multiple strikes. These are often severe wounds resulting in death. The motive is likely feeding or antagonistic behavior rather than mistaken identity.

The "Sneak" Attack: A series of vicious strikes with no warning bump.

Profile of the average shark victim

The longer you spend in shark-infested waters, the higher your chance of being attacked. For this reason, males between the ages of 18 and 35 who spend a lot of time surfing and swimming along the coast of Florida are the most likely to have an encounter with a shark.

A Shark Attack Story

Hilton Mantooth, a 16-year-old surfer, was never really concerned about being bitten by a shark, even though he was swimming in shark-infested waters. "Sure. I've seen them out there. I've even been chased, but my friends and I didn't really think about it," he said. On one fateful day, Hilton and his friends were surfing the inlet at New Smyrna Beach, Fla. He was sitting on his board with his feet dangling in the water when what he thinks was a blacktip shark attacked him from underneath. The shark bit his foot twice before deciding that he wasn't a meal. Hilton says, "I'll definitely get back in the water as soon as I can. The shark was just doing what animals do— feeding. They need to be respected. After all, I was in their home."

GREAT WHITE SHARK

(Carcharodon carcharias)

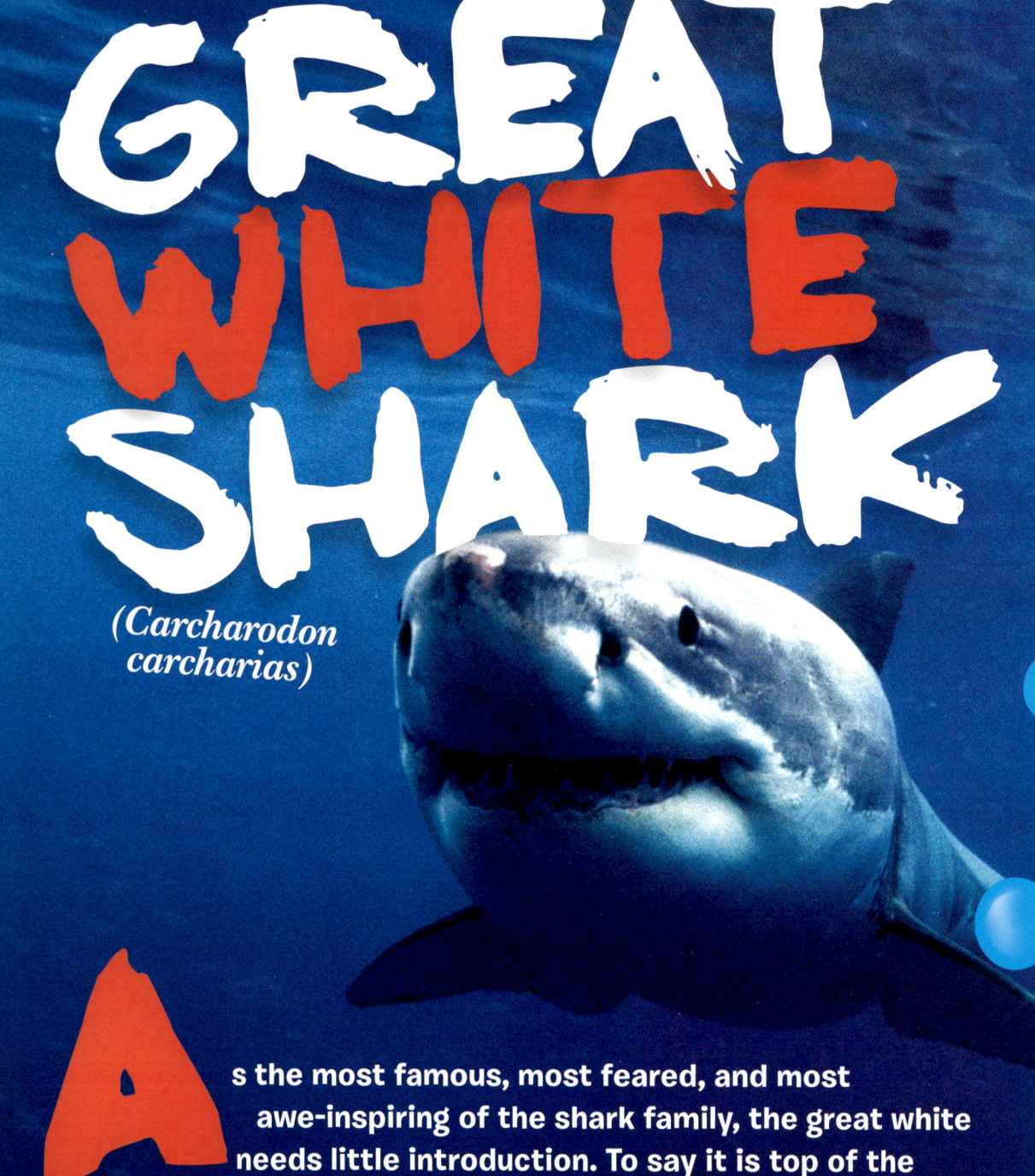

As the most famous, most feared, and most awe-inspiring of the shark family, the great white needs little introduction. To say it is top of the food chain is an understatement. The largest predatory fish on the planet is a lean, mean killing machine. Averaging 15 ft (5 m) in length and reaching speeds up to 35 mph (50 kmh), the great white's equally impressive brain coordinates brute force with sensory information to take down its prey of choice. New research shows the great white is more social than was believed. Complex relationships exist between sharks that humans are only beginning to understand.

Great whites may be the most frightening shark, but they are not the largest. That honor goes to the whale shark (Rhincodon typus), which averages 45 ft (14 m) in length and weighs around 47,000 lbs (21.5 mt). That's one BIG fish!

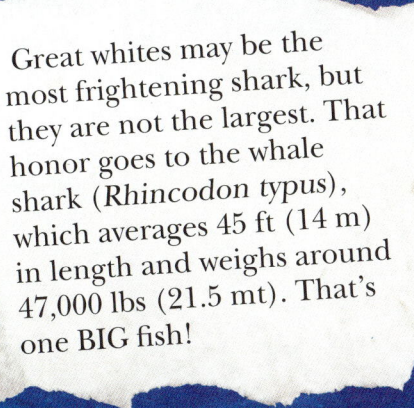

With a single bite, a great white can take in up to 31 lbs. (14 kg) of flesh!

Claim to Fame:
Biggest threat to humans

Size:
Average length: 13-17 ft (4-5 m)
Average weight: 4,000-7,000 lbs (680-1,100 kg)

Body Count:
Total attacks: 279
Fatal attacks: 78

Distinguishing Characteristics:
Great whites have a gray to gray-brown upper body and white belly. They have large, serrated, triangular teeth.

Habitat:
Worldwide in temperate and subtropical oceans, with a preference for cooler waters; inshore waters around rocky reefs and islands, and often near seal colonies.

Diet:
Marine mammals, fish, sea birds

Hunting Style:
The "spy-hopping" technique involves lifting its head above the water to look for prey. Approaching its prey from below at speeds up to 35 mph (50 km) per hour, the great white partially or completely clears the water, a behavior known as breaching. Disabling its prey with the first powerful bite, the great white retreats until the victim is weakened from blood loss, then returns to devour the remains.

Natural Predators:
Orca

Lifespan:
70+ years

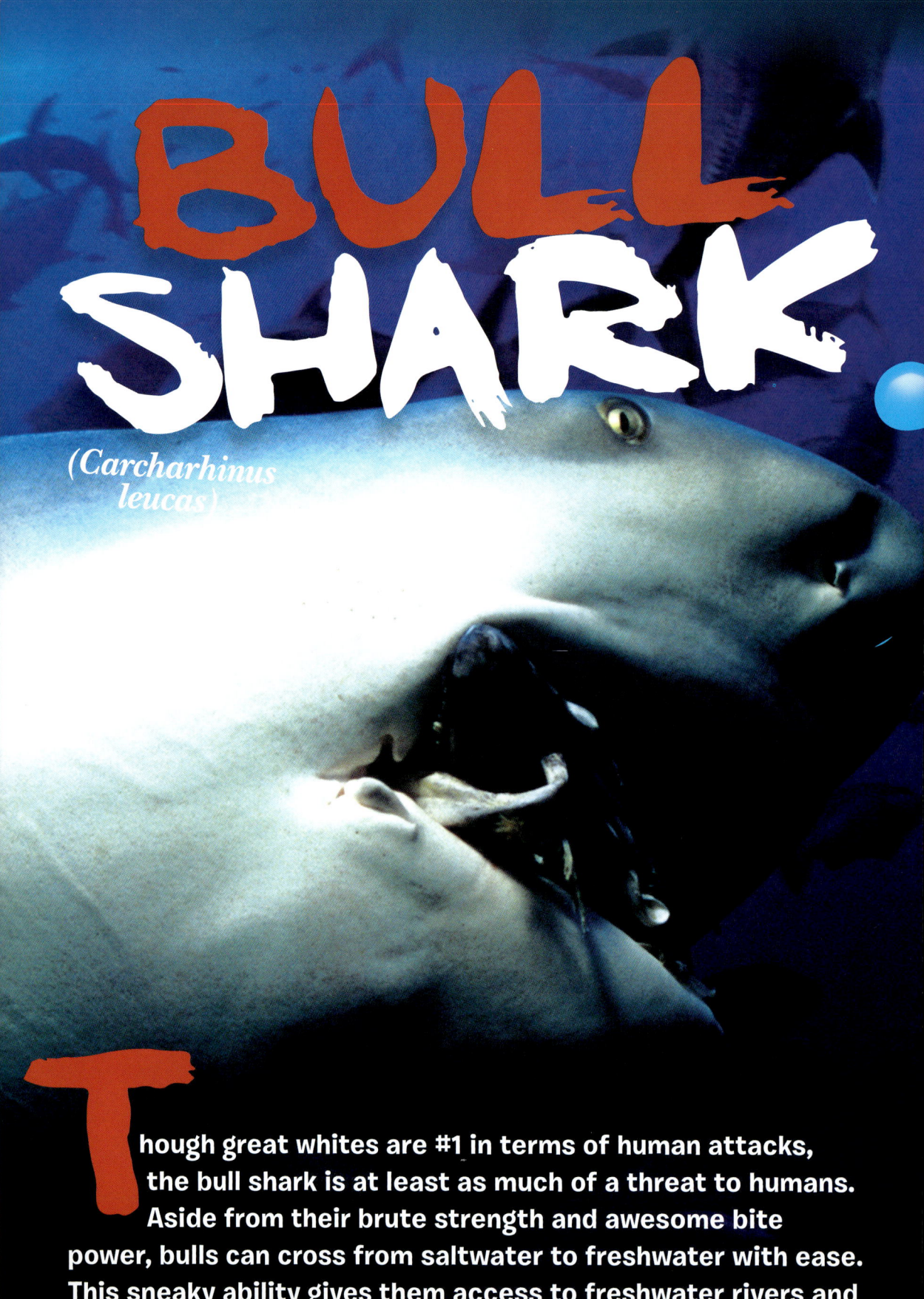

BULL SHARK
(Carcharhinus leucas)

Though great whites are #1 in terms of human attacks, the bull shark is at least as much of a threat to humans. Aside from their brute strength and awesome bite power, bulls can cross from saltwater to freshwater with ease. This sneaky ability gives them access to freshwater rivers and estuaries where humans aren't expecting them, contributing to a high number of unprovoked attacks.

Bite marks from bull sharks have been found on hippopotamuses in Africa's Zambezi River. They are fearless!

Claim to Fame:
Freshwater/saltwater switch hitter

Size:
Average length: 7.5 ft (2.2 m)
Average weight: 209-290 lbs (95-130 kg)

Body Count
Total attacks: 93
Fatal attacks: 67

Distinguishing Characteristics:
"Bull" comes from their stocky shape, blunt snout, small eyes, and aggressive, unpredictable behavior.

Habitat:
Worldwide in the warm shallow waters around coasts and rivers, freshwater estuaries and rivers, and brackish shallows.

Diet:
Bony fish and other sharks (including other bull sharks), turtles, birds, dolphins, terrestrial mammals, crustaceans, and stingrays

Hunting Style:
Bulls are primarily solo hunters. They prefer to attack in murky water so their prey cannot see them coming. The "bump-and-bite" method is often used.

Natural Predators:
Tiger sharks, great whites, larger bull sharks, saltwater crocodiles

Lifespan:
12-16 years

Bull sharks will throw up their stomach contents to distract predators. As the predator moves in to eat the regurgitated food, the bull shark has an opportunity to escape.

11

TIGER SHARK

(Galeocerdo cuvier)

The tiger shark is known for the variety of its diet. Some sharks are picky eaters, focusing their efforts on seals and other favorites, but not the tiger shark. Plump sea bird or tin can, juicy squid or suit of armor—it's all in a day's lunch for a tiger shark! In addition to being a voracious eater, the tiger shark prowls a broad range of habitats—shallow reefs, harbors, and canals—increasing the potential for human encounters.

Claim to Fame:
Garbage can of the sea

Size:
Average length: 12 ft (4 m)
Average weight: 849–1,400 lbs (385–635 kg)

Body Count:
Total attacks: 101
Fatal attacks: 28

Distinguishing Characteristics:
Dark black spots and vertical stripes down the body.

Habitat:
Worldwide in temperate and tropical waters, with the exception of the Mediterranean Sea. Murky waters in coastal areas and open oceans.

Diet:
Crustaceans, marine mammals, fish, jellyfish, squid, turtles, sea snakes, smaller sharks, various inedible man-made items

Hunting Style:
The tiger shark circles its prey and investigates by prodding it with its snout. When attacking, the shark often eats its prey whole, although larger prey is eaten in large bites and finished over time.

Natural Predators:
Larger tiger sharks

Lifespan:
12+ years

Weird Diet

The following items have been found inside the stomachs of tiger sharks:
A polar bear, reindeer, musical instruments, license plates, tires, a chicken coop with chickens, suit of armor, fur coat, barrel of nails, driver's license, porcupine, dogs (some wearing collars), video camera, horse head, bag of money, pigs, sheep, Barbie doll, tools, bottles of wine, 16th-century medallion, cannonball and other live munitions, bag of potatoes, jewelry, pair of pants, empty wallet, hyenas, monkeys, boat cushions, unopened can of salmon, cats, can of peas, human parts.

13

SAND TIGER SHARK

(Carcharias Taurus)

With its wide mouth and haphazard teeth, the sand tiger is known for its deceptively fearsome looks and docile personality. Reluctant to engage with humans unless provoked, the sand tiger is one of the few species of shark able to survive in captivity. Its laid-back personality, menacing appearance, and ability to thrive in captivity makes it the most likely species to be seen in an aquarium.

Claim to Fame:
Shark most in need of orthodontics

Size:
Average length: 6.5–10 ft (2–3 m)
Average weight: 200–350 lbs (90–160 kg)

Body Count:
Total attacks: 29
Fatal attacks: 2

Distinguishing Characteristics:
The sand tiger has a gray-brown back and pale underside. Adults have reddish-brown spots. Long, narrow, sharp teeth impale fish.

Habitat:
Sandy coastal waters, estuaries, shallow bays, and rocky or tropical reefs

Diet:
Small bony fish, rays, skates, squid, crustaceans, smaller sharks

Hunting Style:
Taking a gulp of air at the surface and holding it in its stomach to stay buoyant, the virtually motionless sand tiger silently glides up beside its prey, then attacks with a quick sideways snap. Yikes!

Natural Predators:
Larger sand tiger sharks

Lifespan:
15+ years

A sand tiger shark in captivity

15

BLACKTIP SHARK

(Carcharhinus limbatus)

Fast and energetic, the nimble blacktip is known for leaping above the water and performing multiple spins in the air in pursuit of prey. These spins are the spectacular finale of a feeding run. The shark corkscrews through a school of fish grabbing as many fish as it can at a very high speed. The momentum created propels the shark completely out of the water.

Claim to Fame:
  Most acrobatic

Size:
  Average length:
  5-9 ft (1.5–2.7 m)
  Average weight:
  66-220 lbs (30–100 kg)

Body Count:
  Total attacks: 28
  Fatal attacks: 1

Distinguishing Characteristics:
  Named for its black-trimmed fins, the blacktip has a long, pointy snout and distinct white band along its flank.

Habitat:
  Coastal and subtropical waters around the world including brackish waters. Waters less than 100 ft deep (30 m), muddy bays, island lagoons, and drop-offs near coral reefs, mangrove swamps

Diet:
  Small schooling fish, boney fish, rays and skates, smaller sharks, crustaceans, and the odd cephalopod

Hunting Style:
  Blacktips are social and live and hunt in groups. Timid by nature, they become aggressive and competitive around prey resulting in a feeding frenzy.

Natural Predators:
  Larger sharks

Lifespan:
  12+ years

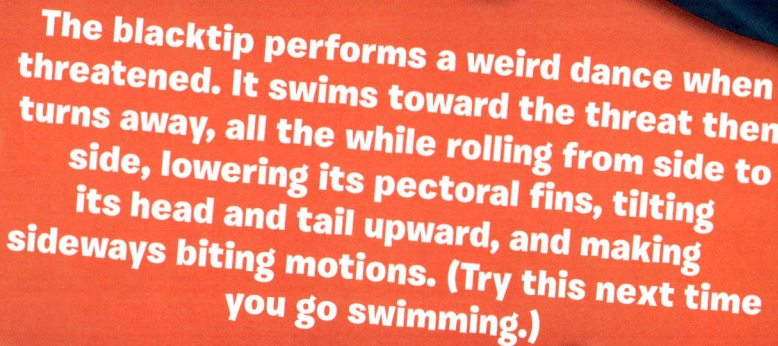

The blacktip performs a weird dance when threatened. It swims toward the threat then turns away, all the while rolling from side to side, lowering its pectoral fins, tilting its head and tail upward, and making sideways biting motions. (Try this next time you go swimming.)

17

GREAT HAMMERHEAD

(Sphyrna mokarran)

Of the nine species of hammerhead sharks, the great hammerhead is the largest. Its unique hammer-shaped head (called a *cephalofoil*) makes it the easiest shark to identify. A solo hunter by night, by day the hammerhead gathers in schools 100-strong.

Claim To Fame:
Weirdest-looking head

Size:
Average length: 13–20 ft (4–6 m)
Average weight: 500–1,000 lbs (230–450 kg)

Body Count:
Total attacks: 21
Fatal attacks: 2

Distinguishing Characteristics:
Large size, flat rectangular head, prominent dorsal fin.

Habitat:
Continental shelves and lagoons in coastal, warm, temperate, and tropical waters

Diet:
Stingrays, fish, squid, octopus, crustaceans, other sharks and even their own young

Hunting Style:
The hammerhead swims directly above the ocean floor, swaying its flattened head from side to side in a sweeping motion to detect the electric signature of stingrays hiding beneath the sand. When a ray is located, the hammerhead delivers a hard blow from above, then pins it to the seafloor and chomps off each wing so it can't escape.

Natural Predators:
Larger hammerheads, bull sharks

Lifespan:
20–30 years

The uniquely shaped head is specially adapted to hunt the hammerhead's favorite meal: stingrays. The broad, flat area is densely packed with ampullae of Lorenzini—the sensory receptors all sharks use to detect the electromagnetic impulses of prey. The wide-set eye placement gives the hammerhead a greater range of vision to better scan the ocean floor for stingrays hiding in the sand.

19

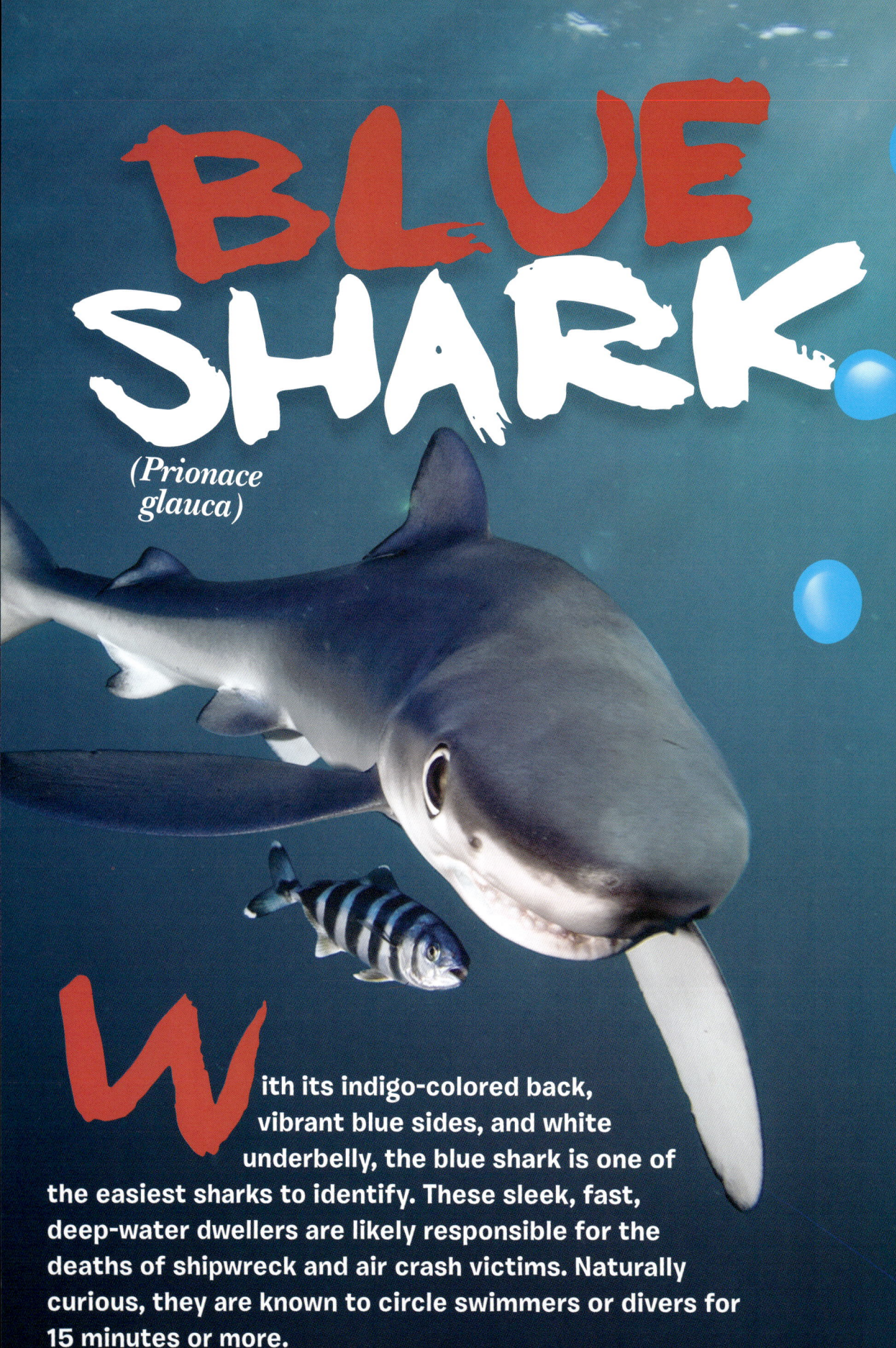

BLUE SHARK
(Prionace glauca)

With its indigo-colored back, vibrant blue sides, and white underbelly, the blue shark is one of the easiest sharks to identify. These sleek, fast, deep-water dwellers are likely responsible for the deaths of shipwreck and air crash victims. Naturally curious, they are known to circle swimmers or divers for 15 minutes or more.

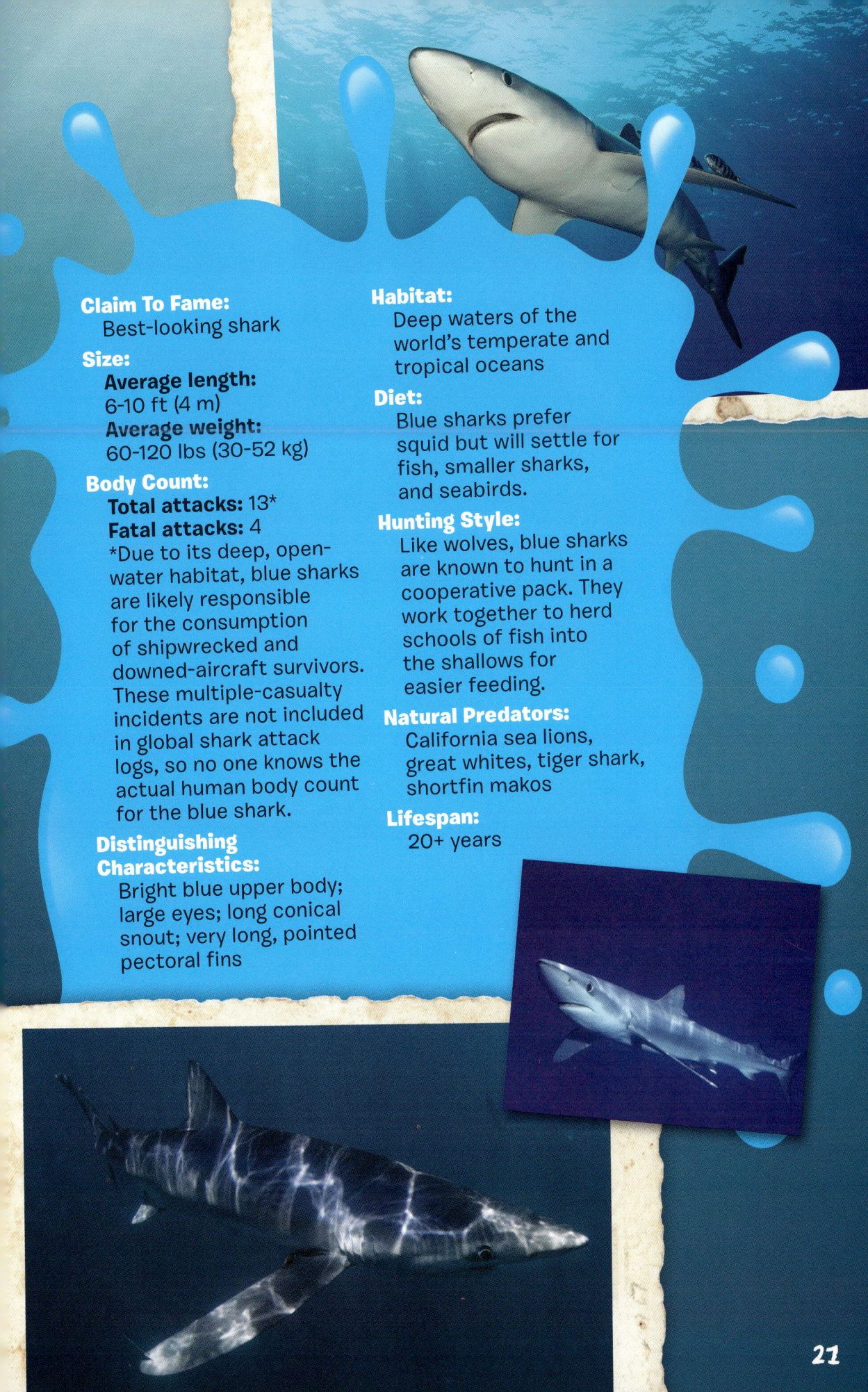

Claim To Fame:
Best-looking shark

Size:
Average length:
6-10 ft (4 m)
Average weight:
60-120 lbs (30-52 kg)

Body Count:
Total attacks: 13*
Fatal attacks: 4
*Due to its deep, open-water habitat, blue sharks are likely responsible for the consumption of shipwrecked and downed-aircraft survivors. These multiple-casualty incidents are not included in global shark attack logs, so no one knows the actual human body count for the blue shark.

Distinguishing Characteristics:
Bright blue upper body; large eyes; long conical snout; very long, pointed pectoral fins

Habitat:
Deep waters of the world's temperate and tropical oceans

Diet:
Blue sharks prefer squid but will settle for fish, smaller sharks, and seabirds.

Hunting Style:
Like wolves, blue sharks are known to hunt in a cooperative pack. They work together to herd schools of fish into the shallows for easier feeding.

Natural Predators:
California sea lions, great whites, tiger shark, shortfin makos

Lifespan:
20+ years

BRONZE WHALER
(*Carcharhinus brachyurus*)

The name "whaler" dates back to the 19th century when these sharks would gather around the carcasses of harpooned whales hanging alongside whaling boats.

Claim to Fame:
 The summer swimmer

Size:
 Average length:
 11 ft. (3.3 m)
 Average weight:
 672 lbs (305 kg)

Body Count:
 Total attacks: 30
 Fatal attacks: 1

Distinguishing Characteristics:
 The bronze whaler's slim, streamlined body is a metallic olive-gray color with a pink tinge on the top and white on the bottom. The color darkens slightly toward the fin tips. It has a long, pointed snout and narrow, hook-shaped upper teeth.

Habitat:
 Worldwide in warm, temperate, and subtropical waters and shallow coastline regions, freshwater and brackish areas of large rivers to shallow bays and estuaries

Diet:
 Cephalopods, bony fish, cartilaginous fish

Hunting Style:
 Bronze whalers hunt in groups up to 100.

Natural Predators:
 Larger sharks

Lifespan:
 25–30 years

SHORTFIN MAKO
(Isurus oxyrinchus)

With its dizzying speed, superb jumping abilities, and high intelligence, the mako is a fearsome predator. Reaching cruising speeds of 25 mph (40km) punctuated with bursts up to 46 mph (74 km), the mako can breach the water at heights of 30 ft (9 m) or higher! Angry makos have been known to attack and leap right into boats.

Claim to Fame:
Highest jumper

Size:
Average length:
10–12.5 ft (3–4 m)
Average weight:
672 lbs (305 kg)

Body Count:
Total attacks: 10
Fatal attacks: 1

Distinguishing Characteristics:
Makos have a brilliant, metallic-blue upper body. The shortfin mako can be identified by its white chin and snout. (Longfin makos have a blue chin and snout.)

Habitat:
Open water in temperate and tropical seas worldwide.

Diet:
Cephalopods, bony fish, other sharks, dolphins, seabirds

Hunting Style:
The mako swims below its prey, hovering in its blind spot, then suddenly lunges upward to capitalize on the element of surprise, often breaching the water.

Natural Predators:
Larger makos

Lifespan:
30 years

"Mako" is the Maori word for *shark*.

OCEANIC WHITETIP

(Carcharhinus longimanus)

Can you imagine surviving a shipwreck or plane crash into the ocean, only to be eaten by a shark? Thanks to the whitetip, many such "survivors" quickly become dinner. Like the blue shark, the whitetip lives in open water and is quick to arrive on the scene of a possible meal. Stubborn in their pursuit of prey, whitetips work themselves into a feeding frenzy as they compete for food.

Claim to Fame:
Frenzied feeder

Size:
Average length:
6–10 ft (2–3 m)
Average weight:
370 lbs (168 kg)

Body Count:
Total attacks: 10*
Fatal attacks: 3
*Due to its habit of eating sailors and others lost at sea, there is no accurate body count for the white tip because multiple-casualty incidents are not included in global shark attack logs.

Distinguishing Characteristics:
The whitetip's rounded fins and long, winglike pectoral and dorsal fins are easily identifiable. The fins have white tips that may be mottled.

Habitat:
Open water in temperate and tropical seas worldwide.

Diet:
Cephalopods, bony fish, other sharks, dolphins, seabirds

Hunting Style:
Whitetip feeding methods include biting into groups of fish and swimming through schools of tuna with an open mouth.

Though generally slow-moving, the whitetip will become aggressive in pursuit of prey. With the arrival of more whitetips at the scene, the competitors quickly work themselves into a vicious feeding frenzy.

Natural Predators:
Larger sharks

Lifespan:
Up to 22 years

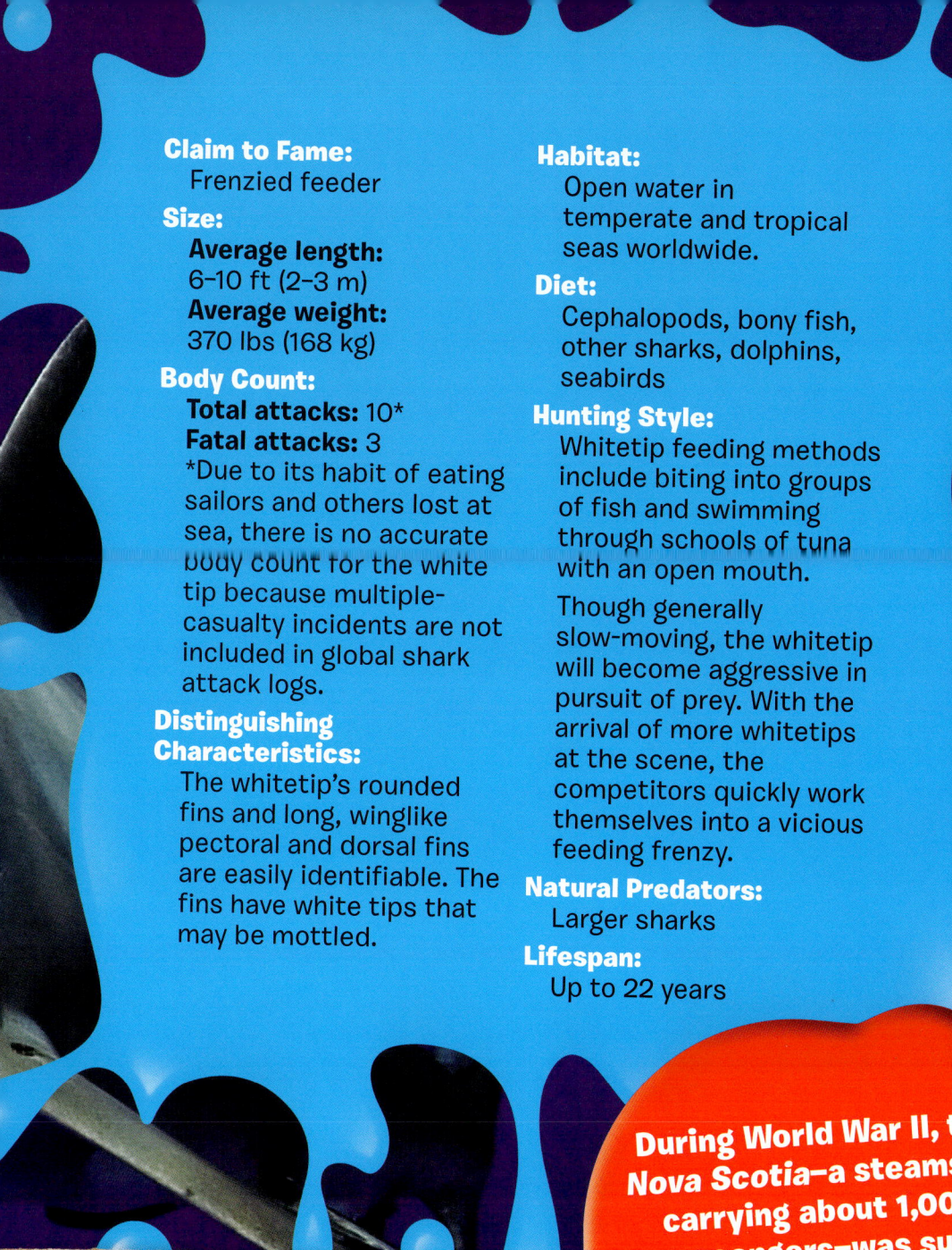

During World War II, the *Nova Scotia*—a steamship carrying about 1,000 passengers—was sunk by a German submarine near South Africa. With only 192 survivors, many deaths were attributed to the whitetip.

ANATOMY OF A SHARK

Teeth
Shark teeth are attached to the gums rather than the jaw. Several backup rows exist so when a tooth is lost, another moves forward immediately to take its place. Shape depends on the shark's diet. Mollusk- and crustacean-eaters have blunt teeth for crushing; fish-eaters have thin, needlelike teeth to spear and grip; and meat-eaters have pointed, triangular-shaped teeth with tiny serrations for ripping through flesh.

Shape
Most shark bodies are rounded in the center and taper at each end like a bullet or torpedo, a hydrodynamic shape that increases speed.

Dermal Denticles
A shark's skin is made up of dermal denticles. These are tiny scales similar to teeth. Like teeth, each denticle has a layer of enamel and includes dentine and a pulp cavity. Denticles completely cover the shark's body and act as an external skeleton. Muscles are attached directly to the denticles, which makes them more efficient and saves energy. Denticles streamline the body to improve speed and provide protection from predators.

Fins
Most sharks have four to five fins:

Pectoral: Located near the head, the pectoral fins are used to lift and steer while swimming.

Pelvic: The pelvic fin sits behind the pectoral fin(s) and aids in stabilization.

Dorsal Fin: This is the fin that sticks out of the water when a shark swims close to the surface. It is also used for stabilization.

Anal Fin: Situated on the rear underside of the shark, these fins provide further stabilization.

Caudal Fin: Also called the tail fin, it provides the most thrust to propel the shark through the water. It has upper and lower lobes that vary in shape and size between types of shark. Most of the thrust comes from the top lobe.

Smell is the most important of a shark's senses. Sharks inhale water through their noistils and filter it through the olfactory sacs. Signals sent to the brain allow the shark to determine the presence of prey. It is said the great white can smell one drop of blood in 10 billion drops of water from more than 300 feet (100 m) away.

Gills
Like other fish, sharks breathe with gills instead of lungs. Water enters the shark's mouth and flows over the gills, where oxygen is absorbed into the bloodstream to be pumped throughout the body. The water then exits through five to seven gill slits on each side of the head.

Spiracles
Some sharks have openings above their eyes that draw oxygenated water into their gills. This means the shark can breathe while lying motionless on the sea floor. To keep water flowing over their gills, sharks without spiracles must move continuously.

Ampullae of Lorenzini
Small groups of sensitive cells under the skin in the shark's head detect the vibrations and electrical fields of fish and other prey.

Countershading
The upper half of the shark is dark to blend with the deeper water beneath when viewed from above. The lower half is white so it blends with the lighter water near the surface when viewed from below. This helps disguise the shark from predators and prey.

Nictitating Membrane
This translucent, tough membrane is a third eyelid that covers and protects the eye from damage during attacks. Not all sharks have them. The great white, for instance, must roll its eyes backward in their sockets for protection just before striking.

Lateral Line
This line of sensory cells along the shark's body detects changes in the movement of surrounding water. Erratic water movements indicate the presence of prey.

WHAT'S INSIDE

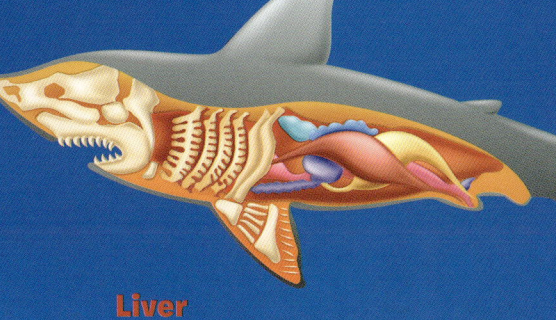

Skeleton
The skeleton of a shark is made of cartilage. This flexible connective tissue allows the shark to bend and twist easily. It is half the weight of bone, which lowers the shark's body mass, meaning less energy is used to propel it through the water.

Liver
A shark's liver is its largest internal organ. The liver stores a lot of oil, which provides an energy reserve between meals. Sharks have been known to survive on their internal oil as long as a year!

Digestion
Food moves from the mouth to the J-shaped stomach, where it can sit for long periods without being digested. Sharks will barf out undigestible items, but some species can completely turn the stomach inside out through their mouth, rinse it with seawater, and return it to its normal inside place.

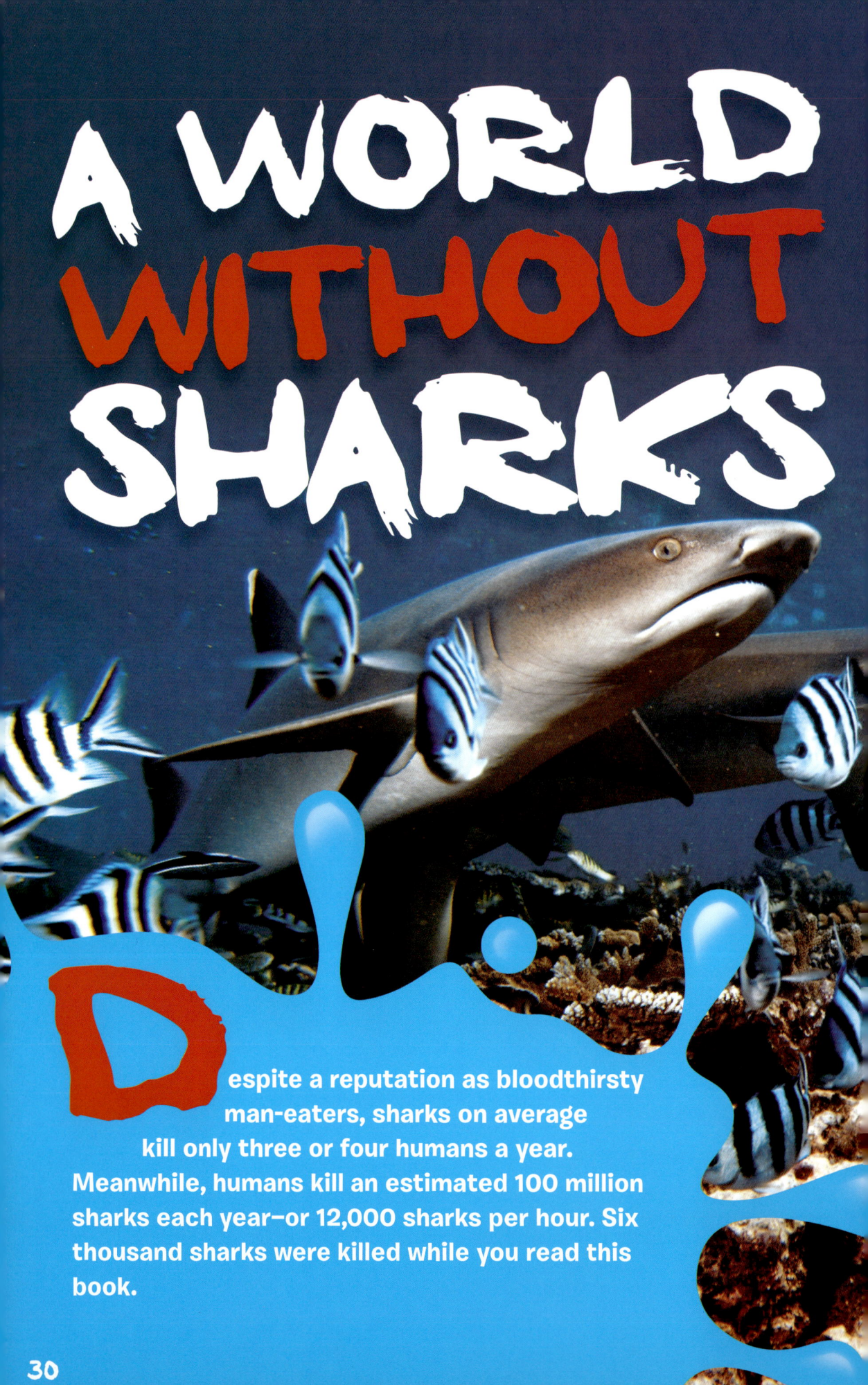

A WORLD WITHOUT SHARKS

Despite a reputation as bloodthirsty man-eaters, sharks on average kill only three or four humans a year. Meanwhile, humans kill an estimated 100 million sharks each year—or 12,000 sharks per hour. Six thousand sharks were killed while you read this book.

Here are some of the reasons:

Overfishing:
Commercial fisheries harvest sharks for their meat and fins.

Sharkfin Soup:
An estimated 75 percent of sharks are killed each year for their fins alone. A symbol of wealth and prosperity, this traditional Chinese soup is served at weddings and special occasions. Because only the fin is valuable to hunters, it is sliced off, and the shark is thrown back into the ocean to die slowly from suffocation or a predatory attack. This horrific method is called *finning*.

Habitat Destruction:
Development and pollution push shark populations out of areas long used for feeding and nurseries.

Skin:
Shark leather is used for purses, bags, shoes, boots, coats, belts, wallets, car interiors, watch straps, gloves, gun holsters, and phone cases.

Bycatch:
Sharks become tangled in the nets, lines, trawls, and fish traps of commercial fisheries.

Sport Fishing and Trophy Hunting:
Due to their size, rarity, and fearsome reputation, sharks are greatly prized by trophy hunters.

Public Aquariums:
A live shark on display makes a lot of money for zoos and aquariums. Sadly, most captive sharks die within a year, even in the most state-of-the-art aquariums.

Public Fear:
Due to media exaggeration of sharks' threat to humans, the fear of sharks among the general population is so great, the mere sighting of a single shark can trigger an extensive cull (hunt) of the local shark population. Sharks also die from getting tangled in the shark barrier nets installed around swimming areas.

GLOSSARY

Apex predator—Predators with no natural predators of their own. They reside at the top of the food chain and have a crucial role in maintaining the health of their ecosystems.

Cartilaginous fish—Fish with a flexible skeleton made of cartilage instead of bone.

ISAF—International Shark Attack File

Serration—Jagged edges on a tooth that improve the ability to slice through meat